TEMPLE OF DAGON

AUTHOR:	**ART DIRECTOR:**	**CARTOGRAPHY:**
James Thomas	Casey Christofferson	Robert Altbauer
EDITOR:	**LAYOUT:**	**FRONT COVER ART:**
Jeff Harkness	Suzy Moseby	Artem Shukaev
5TH EDITION CONVERSION:	**INTERIOR ART:**	**COVER DESIGN:**
Edwin Nagy	Hector Rodriguez and Thuan Pham	Casey Christofferson
	ART FOR VIRTUAL ASSETS:	
	Brandon Sanderson	
	ONLINE PLATFORMS DEVELOPMENT:	
	Sean King	

TABLE OF CONTENTS

TEMPLE OF DAGON

BY JAMES THOMAS

A FIFTH EDITION ADVENTURE FOR 4–6 TIER 2 CHARACTERS

ADVENTURE BACKGROUND

Some knowledge is unfit for man. Yet ever have there been those who seek out the forbidden — the depraved — for the promise of riches and power. Terrible secrets can thus lie in the dark for generations before the foolhardy and ambitious unearth them once again. So too the wizards of the ancient world had among them those who were too ambitious and too unwise. When a cabal of these arcane philosophers migrated afar to establish a research colony apart from their countrymen, they abandoned all remaining restraint against forbidden lore. Their city grew, surrounded by other communities, and included an astrological and religious center several miles away.

Seduced by the promise of secret knowledge and power, they made pacts with wicked beings from beyond this mortal world. But this came at a price. They lost their humanity — morally and even physically — and their colony was destroyed. All the surrounding communities were dragged down with them. Their once great city of Atrotiri now lies wrecked where it sank beneath the waves of the Sinnar Ocean, an all but forgotten legend.

The small settlement of Santhera arose near the site of the disaster. Over the centuries, valuables were salvaged from the waters near the city. The temple site, however, lay unexplored until recently, when a sea medusa named Lycinia made herself mistress of the temple. A devotee of the demon lord Dagon, she sensed the ancient sacredness of the site and re-consecrated the temple to the worship of the "Shadow in the Sea." While exploring a nearby abyss, she encountered a colony of decadent skum languishing in a bizarre underwater metropolis. Her impassioned sermons on the glories of Dagon awakened purpose within their primeval hearts, and they joined her crusade to spread his gospel across the waters. Soon, sinister sea denizens from far and wide arrived, drawn by the rising power of the temple and their hunger for blood. They lodge in the sunken ruins ringing the temple mount, brooding and plotting.

ADVENTURE SUMMARY

The Temple of Dagon is located off a remote island chain in the Sinnar Ocean, 30 miles southwest of the small town of Santhera. It is a dangerous area due to an unusually large gathering of monstrous sea creatures found there. News of this archaeological site — which may still hold ancient artifacts — recently reached a collector who hopes to acquire these valuable ancient treasures. He now seeks to hire adventurers to plunder the long-forgotten temple.

When the characters arrive in Santhera, they learn the location of the temple site — and more. They discover that a cult of Dagon led by a secret priesthood is now active in the area and that the cultists are preying on nearby fisherfolk. Local merfolk communities also fear a mysterious spire rising out of the sea near the temple. As the adventurers approach the site, they glimpse the ancient temple building cresting above the waves and the sunken ruins in the surrounding shallows. A sealed stone spire jutting above the water hides a malevolent occupant but also presents a secret and secure refuge from which the characters can stage their exploration of the ruins. Danger lurks everywhere, and the characters must choose their strategy while raiding the sunken ruins or assaulting the temple. The ruins hold a variety of wicked sea creatures, dangerous hazards, and rare treasures.

Characters must enter the temple sanctuary where they encounter Dagon-worshipping cultists and skum warriors now dedicated to the evil demon prince. They also discover a flesh-warping and soul-twisting infernal machine that, when skillfully used, grants a boon; however, in unskilled hands it can also cause a terrible change. An underwater well in the sanctuary plunges into dark passageways to the chambers of the high priestess, an undersea medusa with coral snake hair. She and her lacedon guards fight a three-dimensional battle in a waterfilled chamber.

If the heroes approach underwater, they might also enter via a hidden sea cave (**Area T-15**) where they encounter aquatic trolls and other evil sea creatures. Worse yet, a visiting black dragon awaits. Delving deeper, they find a sealed vault holding a collection of *ioun stones* left untouched for centuries. Rare underwater equipment, forbidden knowledge, valuable booty, unique treasures and magic items await the plunder! Can the heroes make wise use of what they discover? Or will they too be drawn into a tempting trap of avarice like the ancients of Atrotiri?

A PROFITABLE PROPOSAL

In the city of Castorhage (or another suitable city in your campaign world), a notorious treasure hunter named Cadan Trevethan (**noble**) recently learned of the ruins of the Temple of Dagon. He desperately wants to acquire any arts and valuables from the site, but he knows this expedition is beyond his abilities. He hopes an able group of adventurers might make the trek and return with anything of value.

To that end, he summons the characters (their reputation having preceded them) to a private meeting. Read the following:

Cadan promises to pay in gold and silver (75% in coin or 100% in store credit) for any ancient art and writings the characters might uncover. This includes items and rubbings of bas-reliefs or inscriptions. Cadan provides a roll of waterproof parchment and a special grease marker (usable above and below water) to obtain these. He tells the characters he will negotiate the price of each piece individually once they return. Any other valuables they find are fair salvage, but he offers the same negotiated rates if the characters desire to sell.

Cadan arranges transport for the characters aboard his ship, *The Hurricane*, to and from Santhera. He promises that Captain Blithe will inform them of their destination once they are underway. Privately, Cadan instructs Captain Blithe to keep far from any danger at the temple site; he doesn't want to risk *The Hurricane*, after all. Finally, the captain introduces the characters to Jamal, a young genie (**djinni**). As Cadan's agent, Jamal is authorized to make trade deals and secure any valuables aboard *The Hurricane*.

Jamal offers to swiftly fly recovered treasures to and from the ancient site to the ship while the characters explore the ruins. He also negotiates prices and sells useful equipment and magic items using any store credit the party obtains during the course of the adventure.

On Cadan's orders, Jamal allots each character an advance of 1,000 gp in store credit. While magic items are generally not available in such a remote region, one of each of the following items is kept in a secure location aboard the ship:

Item	Cost
Decanter of endless air	7,250 gp
Bag of holding	5,000 gp
Cloak of the manta ray	7,200 gp
Feather token, fan	200 gp
Feather token, swan boat	450 gp
Gloves of swimming and climbing	6,250 gp
"Kingfisher," a +1 trident	8,000 gp
Necklace of adaptation	9,000 gp
Spell scroll of *greater restoration*	4,000 gp

Additionally, up to 10 units each of the following are available:

Item	Cost
Potion of greater healing	300 gp
Potion of superior healing	750 gp
Potion of fly	750 gp
Potion of water breathing	750 gp

Feel free to add any other item to the lists as you see fit. At the end of the venture, any remaining store credit can be cashed out at 75% in gold and silver.

The Djinni Boy

At 223 years of age, Jamal (**djinni**) is young by genie standards. He resembles a human boy of 12 years with a personality to match, though he somehow is blessed with a wisdom beyond such years. He is only human-sized and tends to avoid combat. He can fly at 90 feet per round and does so invisibly to avoid danger. A thoughtful being by nature, he uses *create food and water* to refresh the party if they run short of food, wine, or other mundane supplies.

Jamal will not suspect any treachery from the characters, which means they can easily hide some of the ancient items they might find at the ruined temple. Even if he finds out, he might not care as he has no affection for Cadan. In his spare time, he amuses himself with a small hookah that he uses to exhale weaves of multicolored mist to form dancing girls, sea serpents, and scenes from home. He has a *carpet of holding* (see **Appendix B: Equipment & Magic Items**) to help tote any valuables the characters want to convert into store credit. He keeps careful track of their credit in a small leather ledger. (You can account for each character's balance by using the credit ledger found in **Appendix C: Accounting Ledger**.)

The Sea Voyage

Add whatever excitement you want to the sea journey, including any sea monsters or random weather events. When you are ready, the characters finally arrive at Santhera.

SANTHERA

The town of Santhera is the only substantial settlement found in this remote area of the Sinnar Ocean. It is a town of about 3,000 people, the vast majority human with several hundred gnomes and halflings and a smattering of elves and dwarves. When *The Hurricane* arrives, the characters see a platform at the mouth of the bay. A galley guides the ship safely into the harbor, avoiding the treacherous obstacles hiding under the surface.

Notable members of Santhera include:

- Percutio Opavian, High Judge (NE male human **noble**)
- Marco Domi, Captain of the Guard (N male human **veteran**)
- Sister Pas, High Priest (LN female human **priest** of Quell)

Thousands of years ago, the island where Santhera now sits was larger and home to the city of Atrotiri. Few specifics are known about Atrotiri, but lore suggests it was founded as a colony of exiled wizards searching for a peaceful bastion in which to research their arcane philosophy. Darker tales are built upon rumors that the Atrotiri performed foul experiments that led to their exile originally, and that they modified these experiments to twist and enslave the creatures of the deep. Whichever is true, all stories agree that Atrotiri was destroyed after the mages dug too deeply into forbidden arts and triggered a massive earthquake that caused much of the island to slide into the sea, leaving behind only the massive crater that now forms Santheran Bay.

The ruins of old Atrotiri now cover the floor of the bay. During extremely low tides, the tips of old bronze spires and the jagged tops of stone walls still peek above the waters, and rich coral and pearl beds cover the submerged ruins. As the island was repopulated over the centuries, locals raised their children to be strong swimmers, sending the best down to dive for treasures. Sometimes, divers find ancient artifacts that collectors, wizards, and their agents are eager to possess. Much of the rest of the economy is simple fishing.

Ostensibly ruled by a town council, the Opavian family has effectively ruled the town for generations. The family keeps a tight grip on the positions of high judge over the island and council leader by nominating their own children, nieces, or nephews before retiring from the posts. Santherans are deeply conservative, though in practice they are largely apathetic. They live quiet lives filled with daily work and seasonal festivals, during which they drink fermented olive juice, just as their parents and grandparents before them.

Rumors at Santhera

Inquisitive characters can learn useful rumors around Santhera with successful Charisma (Persuasion) or Intelligence (Investigation) checks made while talking to the locals. Details of each rumor are found below.

DC	Rumor
12	Bounty
15	Recent Emissaries
18	Piratical Conspiracy
20	The Fang in the Sea

The characters find a notice posted in a public place (see the **bounty poster handout** at the end of the adventure). If they take the notice to the judicial palace, the characters soon find themselves before High Judge Percutio Opavian, who explains the situation and makes them an offer. Merchant vessels have gone missing of late, and indications are that the attacks originate at underwater ruins 30 miles from town. The high judge wants the area investigated immediately and offers a yearlong letter of marque to any adventurers willing to take the bounty. High Judge Opavian pays 50 gp in cash for useful information about the attacks plus an additional 10 gp for the head of each marauder "brought to justice" dead or alive. Santhera is not a wealthy community and cannot afford to pay much. If pressed for more, the high judge offers free provisions including food, ammunition (standard, nonmagical arrows, bolts, and sling bullets), and lodging in the Magocrat, the best (and only) inn in Santhera. Residents are unwilling to accompany the characters to the ruins, and the high judge cannot spare anyone to accompany them.

Captain Blithe will not take *The Hurricane* into hazards beyond Santhera under any circumstances, so the characters must find another way to the island. A successful DC 15 Charisma (Persuasion) check and a bribe of 20 gp convinces a local fisherman named Fodor (**commoner**) to guide them to the site in his small fishing boat, but he won't remain to wait for their return. The party can also purchase a used fishing boat for 50 gp if they have no other means of traveling the 30 miles across the sea.

The djinni Jamal will carry treasure to and from the ruins for them, but he won't assist the characters in getting there.

Recent Emissaries

Local **merfolk** visited Santhera several weeks ago and reported that organized bands of sahuagin and other wicked sea denizens had launched raids on their outlying communities. The raiders were well-equipped and used strange magic. Scouting parties concluded that the raiders seemed to originate from the underwater ruins and the ancient temple. They can serve as guides to the temple and, if questioned, can identify the Fang in the Sea. They know very little about the temple, though they can introduce the characters to Namara. The merfolk avoid combat and hastily retreat if threatened or attacked.

Piratical Conspiracy

The characters overhear the following conversation when they are in a crowded tavern or at the Magocrat.

> The voice of a fisherman near you draws your attention. He straddles a chair and faces away from you, conversing with a group of friends at his table. He drinks his fill and slams the mug down on the table before he speaks. "If you ask me, it's none other than the high judge behind the raids on the trade ships. He's enriching himself and his friends, depriving us and blaming it on outsiders."
>
> The patron to his right nods in agreement. "Aye, Dubio. Why do you think there's that strange ship in the harbor? *The Hurricane*? And those crude mercenaries stomping around? The judge is preparing to put down any resistance to his rule if word gets out that he's involved."

A successful DC 20 Intelligence (Investigation) check reveals this to be a false rumor. Although there certainly is corruption in the local government, the high judge is not responsible for the raids and genuinely desires to end the attacks lest the town's supplies suffer.

The Fang in the Sea.

While gathering information, the characters encounter Namara (elf **priest** with Strength 14, Athletics +4, and *helm of water breathing* [see **Appendix B: Equipment and Magic Items**]), who insists on meeting the whole party so she can share the following:

> "Since monsters destroyed my village 800 years ago, I have resided in a nearby merfolk village. The gods of the seafolk heard my desperate prayers and sent me a vision of off-islanders defeating the evil that attacked my people."

After sharing her story, she requests their help protecting her community. She tells them about the Fang in the Sea and asks them to expunge that evil. If they agree, she continues:

> "A black granite pinnacle juts from the sea 30 nautical miles southwest of Santhera. The fisherfolk call it the Fang in the Sea. It marks the periphery of the sunken remains of an ancient city lost long ago beneath the waves. Evil waits there."

Namara directs the characters to the spire or she accompanies them if asked, although she will not enter the temple.

THE OBSERVATORY SPIRE

An ancient temple to a forgotten god crests above the waves 30 nautical miles from Santhera, perched upon what must have been the highest hill in the former city. This is the location Cadan hired the characters to investigate. The spire is made of nearly seamless thick granite and has no obvious entrance.

However, if Namara accompanied the characters, she tells them that she was one of five adventurers who gained entrance to the spire long ago. Their astrologer Shalell and the historian Feloor found a doorway near the top of the spire and opened it one dark night almost 800 years ago. But she warns the characters of a terrible ghostly girl who slew her companions and turned them into evil spirits. Nevertheless, if the characters destroy the undead denizens, the shelter would be a secure place to rest between forays into the temple or the underwater ruins, for it is nigh impregnable.

At night, glowing runes on the side of the spire are visible by starlight or moonlight. The runes begin to glow one after another as the moon and stars rise. If each rune is traced in that same sequence, a stone doorway recedes inward and sinks into the floor to reveal an ornate star chamber. Once the pattern is known, the door can be opened day or night by retracing the runes. However, the outside runes and the opening are 10 feet above the sea's surface at high tide, so characters might need to climb or use some sort of magical assistance to reach them.

If Namara is still with the characters once the door is opened, she avoids combat and refuses under any conditions to enter the tower. If monsters attack, she jumps into the water and flees.

THE OBSERVATORY SPIRE'S HISTORY

Jorell the Stargazer locked his young daughter, Ismene (*iz'-meh-nay*), in the tower to protect her from the disaster he knew would befall the city. Alas, his inattention over the years had already planted seeds of bitterness that their abrupt parting caused to spring up full blown, paying tragic dividends. After the city sank, killing nearly everyone including her whole family, Ismene was left all alone and unable to escape the observatory spire. As the darkness closed in, she gave in to her bitterness and anger, blaming her father for her predicament and for every awful thing that had ever happened to her. She smashed every object she could find, tore up books, and damaged furniture. In the end, still bitter and resentful, she died of hunger and became a terrible **wraith**. The spire also contains her three spawn (**specters**), undead corruptions of Namara's companions who entered the spire long ago.

The spire, one of the most revered buildings in the ancient city, is quite solidly built and completely intact. Presently, the interior is unlit unless otherwise stated. The floors, walls, and ceilings are made of dark granite and ornate marble. Amazingly, most furnishings are still in one piece. If cleared of evil spirits, this ancient building could indeed provide a safe and secure hideout for the adventurers. If they are careful not to be observed withdrawing to this location, the temple's denizens may never find them. And even if the characters are seen, their foes have no way of getting inside (none knows the secret of tracing the runes). Even Jamal the djinni can't enter the spire unless it is opened for him. The characters can use the crystal sphere in the divination chamber (**Area S-2**) to view the outside world to see who's there. They can open the door from the inside at any time, day or night.

S-1. OBSERVATORY

Precise gaps in the stone lattice above allow viewers to track the movement of various stars and constellations, measure the passage of time, take astrological readings, and view portents from beyond. The room is otherwise vacant.

A secret counterweight and lever allow those inside the chamber to open and close the observatory's door from the inside. The lever can be found with a successful DC 20 Wisdom (Perception) check. It takes two rounds to close and seal the spire. Besides opening and closing the secret entrance, the ancient astrologers could also retract and close openings in the walls and roof, and even rotate them to align the room with a variety of celestial constellations. The devices for these movements are missing, however, and the magical energies that powered them are long dormant.

The hole in the middle of the floor is all that remains of a magical elevator that ran from the top of the spire to the bottom. A stone levitating table the ancients stood upon now lies in pieces at the bottom of the shaft. The descent to the level below therefore requires a character to jump, fly, use magic, or descend by rope. It's a 15-foot drop to the next floor down. Characters can hang from the upper level and drop safely down with a successful DC 14 Dexterity (Acrobatics) check. With a successful check, the character takes no damage and lands safely on the next level down. On a failed check the characters lands successfully but is knocked prone and takes 3 (1d6) bludgeoning damage. A character who fails the check by 5 or more misses the edge of the floor below and falls to the bottom of the shaft, taking 3 (1d6) bludgeoning per 10 feet fallen. Each level is 15 feet from floor to floor and the fall alerts the monsters on each level as the character goes past.

Loud noises in this area attract monsters in the room below.

S-2. DIVINATION CHAMBER

Lurking here are 3 **specters**. Ismene gave them names: Bitterness, Envy, and Vengeance. If they hear voices from the floor above, they fly up to attack. Otherwise, they hide in the walls and try to forget the undead horrors they have become.

The last intact globe is three feet wide and filled with pure elemental water. Spellcasters can use it as a scrying device. If properly identified with a successful DC 18 Intelligence (Arcana) check or suitable magic, it operates as a *crystal ball*. It is encased in its metal stand, which is attached to the floor. Removing it is impossible without breaking it. No other valuables are in this room.

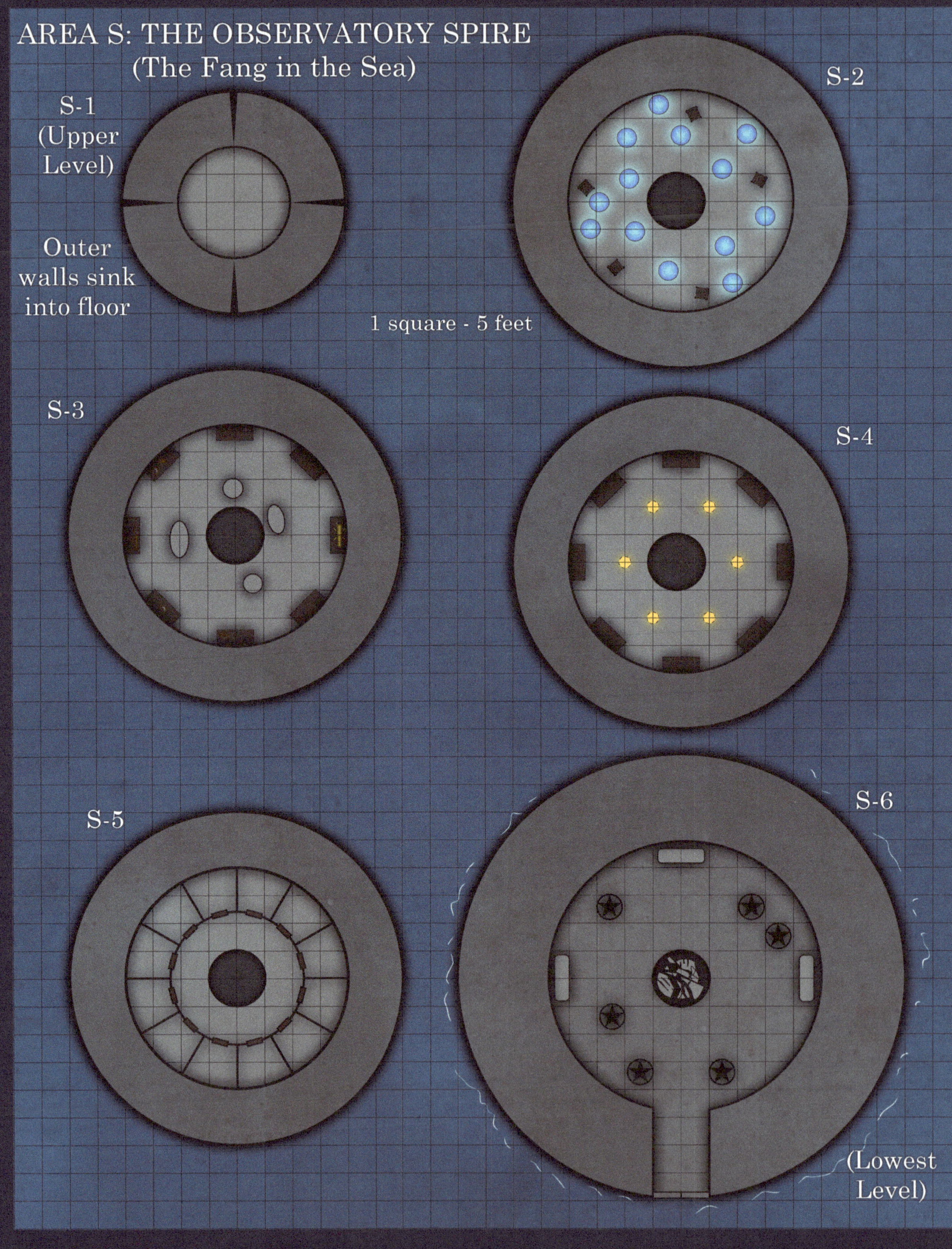

AREA S: THE OBSERVATORY SPIRE
(The Fang in the Sea)
S-1
(Upper
Level)
S-2
Outer
walls sink
into floor
1 square - 5 feet
S-3
S-4
S-5
S-6
(Lowest
Level)

S-3. Central Equipment Storage

A variety of astrological instruments are in this room, from magnifying glasses to telescopes, and compasses to astrolabes. There are tools for basic maintenance and spare lenses and other parts in handy drawers. The ancient artifacts found here are worth 12,000 gp, and Jamal happily receives them as recovered "art" and credits the characters' account accordingly.

S-4. Scriptorium

For this encounter, identify five or six squares of rough terrain on the map to represent the chaos of Ismene's angry rampage so many centuries ago. Strangely afraid of the intruders, Ismene (**specter**) hides inside a random bookcase. She flies into a rage and attacks if she hears a man's voice, as this reminds her of her hated father.

Most of the books here are on scrolls, and most of them were torn to shreds long ago. They are all written in ancient languages from more than 3,000 years ago. No magic books or scrolls are present, but the ancient writings that can be recovered are worth 9,000 gp. Ismene's physical remains — a girl's emaciated body — are huddled in a corner.

S-5. Dormitory

A key hangs behind each door on a cloak hook. A simple bed with a mattress on a bronze bed frame is inside each cell. A chamber pot is beneath each mattress. An ever-burning lantern hangs from the ceiling on a bronze chain. The lantern can be opened and closed to provide bright, dim, or no light. A desk and chair sit in one corner. Otherwise, each room is empty.

S-6. Entrance Hall

The stone doors can be opened only after disabling the lock in the wall by the side of the door and then pulling a lever. The lock consists of three metallic concentric circles and can be deciphered with a successful DC 22 Intelligence (Investigation) check. Opening the door is a grave error for the fool who does so, however. As the stone doors recedes into the floor, water gushes into the tower with great force, flooding **Areas S-3** through **S-6** and filling half of **Area S-2**. Each creature in the room must make a DC 16 Strength saving throw, taking 14 (4d6) bludgeoning damage on a failure or half as much on a success.

THE LOST CITY

The core of this adventure takes place at the temple, but enterprising players may want to explore around the underwater ruins for monsters and treasure. Make the ruins as elaborate or as simple as desired depending on the interests of your gaming group. Mark which encounters you wish to include and keep a tally of what monsters remain. Rather than having them quit the region, the surviving monsters could flee to the temple to be encountered anew in the pilgrims' hostel (**Area T-12**).

Review the rules for Underwater Combat and adjustments for movement. Before the characters enter the water, review each character's ability to breathe underwater and any movement adjustments. Visibility is quite good in these clear waters, so the only restrictions are light and obstacles. Almost all the monsters here are aquatic with swim speeds. Remember the three-dimensional aspect of the environment enables attacks to come from above and below.

THE SUNKEN RUINS

Below are four encounter areas that can be placed anywhere in the sunken ruins. Choose encounters that allow your players to show off their characters' special abilities and keep them interested in the adventure. You don't have to use them all, but if you want more, you can use the **Random Sunken Ruins Encounters** table below to spice things up. The shallow seawaters here range between 20 to 60 feet below the surface. During the day, the water is clear enough that characters can see the ruined buildings about 40 feet below the surface. You could use any convenient city street maps you have handy and dress them up as ruins. Players may enjoy having their characters swim over walls and rooftops on previously used flip maps. Organize encounters in the sunken ruin by placing encounters where they make sense to you. The remainder of the ruins should be empty shells of buildings or rubble.

Monsters in the ruins are awaiting their next marauding mission, but they attack if they detect intruders. Swimming or boating in plain sight is a good way to get clobbered by the bad guys. If the party takes reasonable precautions to avoid being detected by residents of the ruins, reward them with limited or no random encounters. If, however, they boldly and blatantly swoop in like flying superheroes, they have chosen a path of pain. Use the **Random Sunken Ruins Encounters** table below and show no mercy as the denizens below spot them and attack. As more monsters get word of the characters' presence, they attack in waves and alert the temple for backup. You obviously don't want to punish your players if they realize too late what they've gotten into. The game can still be saved; as things heat up, give them hints and opportunities to retreat and regroup. Remind them that they were told this area is likely a hub of the recent attacks and that monsters are certainly lurking in the ruins.

RANDOM SUNKEN RUINS ENCOUNTERS

1d12	Result
1	2d4 **caryatid column** guardians*
2	4 **skum** warriors (from **Area T-5**)*
3	3d6 **skum** pilgrims*
4	2d6 **sahuagin**
5	Crystal ooze (as **grey ooze**)
6	**Spirit naga** (aquatic)
7	1d4 **allips** (ghosts of ancient city)*
8	**Storm giant**, evil, Dagon-worshipping
9	1d3 + 1 **lacedons** (aquatic ghouls)*
10	2 aquatic **trolls** (from **Area T-8**)
11	Dagon **priests** (from **Area T-4**)
12	**Eye of the deep***

*see **Appendix A**

R-1. Mall Prison

Read the following if the characters enter:

This two-story complex was once part of a vast indoor bazaar. Now, the shops are makeshift cells for captives taken in recent raids. The central passage is 30 feet wide and 70 feet long before it makes a sharp turn that ends in rubble. Cells are located every 10 feet or so along the passage. The ruined roof is mostly intact but a search with a successful DC 13 Wisdom (Perception) check from above the building reveals an opening in the back around the eastern corner where characters could sneak inside.

Manning this area at all times are 10 **skum** (see **Appendix A**), with two at the entryway and the remainder at the back. They are bored with their duties and fill the empty hours with an underwater ballgame called "lathoosh," a three-player game with racquets and a ball very much like a mix of lacrosse and tennis. They also enjoy terrorizing the merfolk with monstrous eels. Thus, they may be unaware of approaching characters if they quietly slay the two skum at the entrance. If hard pressed, they release the eels to join the fight.

The net contains 2 **giant moray eels** (see **Appendix A**). They attack if one of the prison guards uses an action to release them. Awaiting their fate as blood sacrifices to Dagon are 14 **merfolk** who are attached to the walls by bronze shackles. One of them, Jahwass (**noble** with a swim speed of 40 ft. and the ability to breathe underwater), is of noble birth. A reward arrives at Santhera for the characters three days after his safe return: a box of rare pearls (2,000 gp) and a *trident of fish command*. A locked box nearby holds the merfolk equipment and weapons. The keys to the manacles and strongbox hang on a peg near the entrance.

R-2. The Hag Garden

See the Hag Garden map for this encounter.

A coven of 2 **sea hags** and a **green hag** (who form a coven) constructed this garden of monstrous flora to amuse themselves. They consider it high art and are quite conceited about their creation. All the creatures therein obey their commands. The cavorting merfolk are actually 6 zombie merfolk (as **zombies** with a swim speed of 50 feet) covered by illusions. The illusion can be pierced with a successful DC 17 Intelligence (Investigation) check. They continue their circuit from one end of the garden to the other and merely smile and nod to any who address them. The remaining monsters do not appear to be dangerous unless examined closely with a successful DC 18 Intelligence (Nature) check. The groves on either side of the garden each contain a patch of monstrous kelp (as **assassin vines**, see **Appendix A**) that attack those who stray too close (reach five feet). Throughout the garden are 4 **giant sea anemones** (see **Appendix A**) that attack creatures as large as the characters only if a hag commands them to do so. Several varieties of poisonous undersea plants are carefully cultivated here for nefarious purposes. Address these only if the characters take interest in them.

Tactics

If taken alone or one or two at a time, the monsters in the garden are no match for a party of 6th-or 8th-level characters. Therefore, use this encounter area to fit your player's progress. If they need a greater challenge, the zombies attack the frontline characters when they enter the garden while the sea anemones move up on backline characters. Maybe throw in an assassin vine attack if any characters move too close to the side lawns. Remember that assassin vines can animate other vines in the area. You can make them poisonous plants for an added danger.

The hags are out of sight in the ruined palace gnawing on the carcass of their most recent merfolk plaything, but they notice if a disturbance occurs in the garden. Once the characters are engaged in the garden, the three hags appear together as mermaids in Round 2 and begin casting spells. If attacked, the sea hags drops the illusion and use the sea hag's horrific appearance as they concentrate melee attacks on one opponent at a time.

If the party needs an easier challenge, break up the monster encounters. Consider bringing the hags in one round at a time along with one other garden monster threat. Avoid new monster attacks from behind.

The animated dead fish swim about for artistic effect and are not dangerous enough to count as a monster. However, you could turn them into weak zombies to threaten backline spellcasters. The octopus zombie could be an easy kill as the characters are searching for treasure as it does not stop operating the fountain.

The hags have the following valuables on their persons: a bag of 20 adamantine sling bullets, a potion *of gaseous form*, a potion *of water breathing*, and a potion *of mind reading*. Three of the merfolk wear valuable jewelry (total value 600 gp). If the fountain area is searched with a successful DC 15 Wisdom (Perception) check, a giant oyster is found behind the fountain. This three-foot-wide mollusk is not dangerous, but if pried open with a DC 18 Strength check, a valuable pearl is found within (700 gp). Lastly, three silver coins are in the fountain.

R-3. Shrine of Insanity

This shrine to a forgotten alien god bears a terrible curse. The skum marked the underground entrance with a warning sign: two driftwood planks formed into an "X" with a downward pointing scallop shell in the middle, the skum sign for "Danger! Do not enter!"

The temple chamber is 20 feet wide, 10 feet high, and 40 feet long. The area is bare except for the seven-foot-tall golden idol at the rear of the sanctuary. The pit in the middle of the room is an old trap sprung long ago by a looter whose skeletal remains lie amid broken tiles 40 feet down. A **gibbering mouther** slumbers under rubble in a corner of the pit. It can be detected with a successful DC 18 Wisdom (Perception) check. It is sensitive to vibrations and awakens and attacks immediately if the rubble

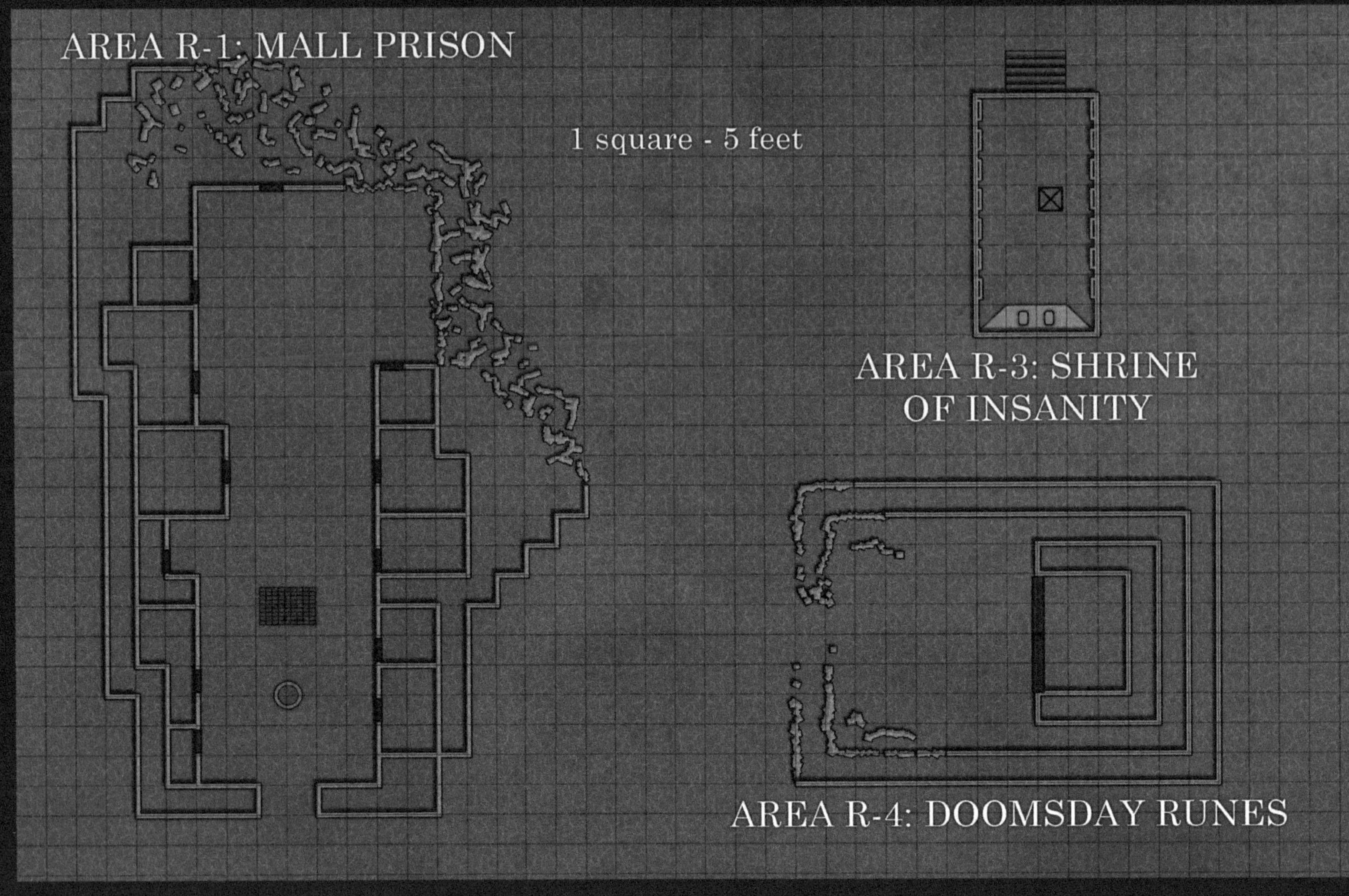

or bones are disturbed. A second mouther dozes behind the statue (same Perception chance to detect) but awakens and attacks if it detects noises or bright light.

Anyone touching the idol feels a vibration thrum through their body and must succeed on a DC 16 Constitution saving throw or fall under a terrible curse. The cursed creature assumes an amorphous, shapeless mass. Its body melts and flows, leaving the creature unable to hold or use any item such as clothing, armor, helmets, and rings. Larger items such as backpacks and armor reduce the target's Dexterity score by 4. Speed is reduced to the lesser of one-quarter normal or 10 feet. The target gains the amorphous quality and cannot cast spells or use magic items. It attacks blindly and cannot distinguish friend from foe. It as disadvantage on all attacks.

The target loses 1 point of Wisdom each round that it ends its turn in an amorphous shape. Upon reaching 1 Wisdom, the victim transforms over four agonizing rounds into a gibbering mouther at full hit points. If the target's Wisdom is raised above 2 during this final transformation, the creature returns to an amorphous state. Only *resurrection* or *limited wish* can reverse the transformation once it is complete.

The cursed target can attempt a DC 15 Wisdom saving throw at the end of each of its turns prior to being transformed into a gibbering mouther. A successful save lets the creature resume its normal form for one minute. Spells such as *alter self*, *polymorph*, *shapechange*, and *stoneskin* that change the target's shape hold the creature in a stable form and prevent Wisdom drain for the duration of the spell. These spells do not end the curse, however.

If the idol is pulled down, it smashes into several pieces on the floor. The idol is hollow with clay over a metal frame. The evil magic is no longer a danger. The small body of a long-dead young person is found inside the statue. Based on the construction, this was a sacrifice who died horribly to consecrate the idol when the clay was fired. The gold leaf covering the outside is difficult to recover and not worth much (50 gp). The rubies and emeralds covering the idol are worth 5,200 gp.

R-4. DOOMSDAY RUNES

As the characters continue through the ruins, a blue glow pulses in the waters around them as they pass a crumbling building. Read the following:

> A blue glow from the ruins of a nearby building softly illuminates the underwater city. The light pulses like a beating heart that ripples the still waters.

The otherwise nondescript building contains a sizable stone object covered in ancient runes. *Comprehend languages* reveals the words "guardian" and "protection" in the jumble of symbols. One side of the stone has a flat palm-size indentation discolored from use. If a character foolishly places his or her hand in the indentation, the runes on the stone illuminate and hum. Doing so activates an ancient city guardian tasked to destroy intruders. Since no citizens are left to control the guardian, it targets every living thing in sight. With one last pulse of intense blue light, the front of the stone block swings open, and the occupant (as **stone golem**) attacks immediately. The construct pursues characters beyond this building but it cannot swim, which should make this an easier encounter for clever players. Rubbings of the runes are worth 2,000 gp.

AREA R-2: THE HAG GARDEN
1 square - 5 feet
Street
Fountain
Ruins
Alley
Kelp
Kelp
Street
Promenade
Street
Alley
Ruins
Sea grass
Sea grass
Ruins
Ruined Palace
Statue
Anemone

Optional Sunken Ruin Dangers

If you need more encounters in the sunken ruins, the following list of dangers can enhance the **Random Sunken Ruins Encounters**:

Collapsing Building

Some ruined buildings may be dangerously unstable. A weakened ceiling can be spotted with DC 18 Intelligence (Investigation) check. A creature beneath the ceiling when a loud noise or explosion occurs must make a DC 15 Dexterity saving throw. The creature takes 28 (8d6) bludgeoning damage and is buried on a failure, or half as much and is not buried on a success. A buried creature is restrained and takes 7 (2d6) bludgeoning damage at the beginning of each of its turns. A buried creature can use an action to attempt a DC 15 Strength (Athletics) check to get free, or an adjacent creature can do the same.

Falling Block Trap

A pressure plate or tripwire triggers a 10-foot-square block of stone to fall. Each creature in the area when the block falls must succeed on a DC 16 Dexterity saving throw or take 21 (6d6) bludgeoning damage and be restrained by the block. A creature can free itself with a successful DC 18 Strength (Athletics) check. An adjacent creature can do the same. The trigger for the trap can be detected with a successful DC 17 Wisdom (Perception) check and disarmed with a successful DC 15 Dexterity check made with thieves' tools.

Glyph of Warding

A creature passing through a doorway triggers a *glyph of warding*. When triggered, the glyph erupts with magical energy in a 20-foot-radius sphere centered on the glyph. The sphere spreads around corners. Each creature in the area must make a DC 17 Dexterity saving throw. A creature takes 27 (6d8) lightning damage on a failed saving throw or half as much damage on a successful one. The glyph can be discovered before being triggered with a successful DC 17 Intelligence (Investigation) check.

TEMPLE OF DAGON

T-1 PORTICO

Great columns, each carved from a single piece of rare marble, adorn the outer portico of this imposing temple. The ages have taken their toll, however. Cracks appear in the stonework, and columns lie broken here and there. Seaweed and thick green mosses claw up the steps and walls. Vague carvings on the outer walls depict faded oceanscapes and sea creatures. Stains of black slime distort the carvings.

Most areas are slime-covered and slippery. At night, 2 **skum** temple guards (see **Appendix A**) on opposite porticos watch for interlopers. By day, 2 **priests** keep watch instead (see **Area T-4**). Neither pair tries to conceal themselves, so the party might spot them in time to eliminate the sentinels by stealth. If the guards detect a dangerous group approaching, they warn the guards and priests inside to prepare. If you really want to increase the challenge, 2 **devilfish** (see **Appendix A**) attack from underwater as the party tops the landing. The clamor of combat likely betrays the party's presence and delays their entrance into the temple proper. It also increases the chances that one of the sentinels rushes in and alerts the defenders.

T-2. ENTRYWAY

This vast sanctuary is covered in marble from floor to ceiling. Sea motifs adorn high points on the walls and protrude from corners and archways in baroque fashion. A sunken pool of multicolored marble dominates the middle of the passage. A statue of a sea nymph holding a bow and arrow stands just above the water level at the center of the pool.

This level of the temple is not underwater. The ceiling height is 30 feet. The underwater portion of this complex begins beneath the sanctuary of Dagon (**Area T-5**). The water in the pool is one-foot deep and contains unholy water (80 pints). Good-aligned fey and celestials who start their turn in contact with the water take 2 (1d4) necrotic damage. One who is submerged in the pool takes 10 (3d6) necrotic damage instead. It is otherwise harmless. The sea nymph statue is made of gilded green marble and holds a bronze bow and arrow. Close scrutiny and a DC 16 Wisdom (Perception) reveals that the arrow is not a part of the statue. It is in fact an *arrow of slaying* (dragon) the high priestess placed here as a ruse to hide it in plain sight. A vision revealed to her that a dragon-like creature would soon come to the temple. She purchased the arrow and placed it here in preparation for the expected attack.

T-3. HIGH PRIESTESS'S ROOM

A grotesque idol of unidentified black and green stone grimaces threateningly from a niche. An unusual circular, pool-like piece of furniture sits in the middle of the room. It is made from the skin of a large serpentine creature that has been stuffed and sewn together. The walls are adorned with strange tapestries of undersea construction that give the room a cold, sea-like quality.

This personal shrine is where the high priestess conducts hours-long meditations each evening. The door is thick and locked, but not trapped. It can be opened with a successful DC 18 Dexterity check with thieves' tools or a DC 22 Strength check.

The high priestess is presently in the oratorium (**Area T-7**). The statue by the door is merely another idol of Dagon. It is worth 500 gp if recovered intact but weighs 500 pounds. A beautiful mother-of-pearl screen at the back of the room (1,200 gp) conceals the entrance to a large closet where a variety of vestments and odd temple apparel are kept in storage. These include a crown made of coral (1,800 gp). A covered candelabrum with six orbs filled with glowing greenish liquid gives off light as a torch when uncovered (300 gp). A specially designed "wet chest" that can secure its contents so they are unaffected by the outside watery environment (200 gp) holds nothing. A bookcase contains 62 blocky tablets made of a strange, coral-like material that is very light and easy to engrave on. Etched on all four sides, most of them are writings (in Abyssal) by the oracle herself. They are filled with prophecies and mad musings on the origin and future of various sea races and nations, but there are also several treatises on sea-demons and Dagon in particular. They are worth 2,000 gp to an interested sage and allow a +2 bonus to Intelligence (History or Religion) checks when consulted on Dagonic subjects. A six-foot-long narwhal horn is carved along its four twirling paths with magical scrimshaws. These constitute four magic scrolls: *protection from poison*, *find the path*, *vampiric touch*, and *conjure animals* (giant blowfish only, see **Appendix A**).

WICKED RECONFIGURATION MACHINE

A large calendar stone covers the far wall. It depicts circle upon circle of enigmatic runes with strange green metal coursing between and around them. Two batons of the same metal protrude at chest height, and a pair of foot-shaped indentations are on the stone floor before the mural. In the middle of the bas-relief, a grotesque demonic face — half-fish, half monstrous beast — leers out. Off to the side, wires run from a device in a niche to green metallic bolts on the edge of the mural.

Known by the ancients as the "Flesh and Soul Reconfiguration Contrivance," this device was intended to enable users to permanently modify their physical and mental abilities. In this way they hoped to enhance the vigor of their race. The device is not perfect, and results vary. The user risks receiving a bane rather than a boon (see the chart below). To operate the device, the user stands before the mural and grasps a baton in each hand. With a loud hum, mysterious runes flash in concentric circles for a full round as energies build and take form. To influence the transformation, users may increase their chances of a beneficial result by adding their Charisma or Intelligence modifier to a d20 roll. All transformations have an undersea component to them, i.e. "improved vision" improves sight by giving the user fish-like eyes. Changes are permanent unless noted. Each use consumes three charges from the attached battery. The battery that is currently connected has only 10 charges remaining.

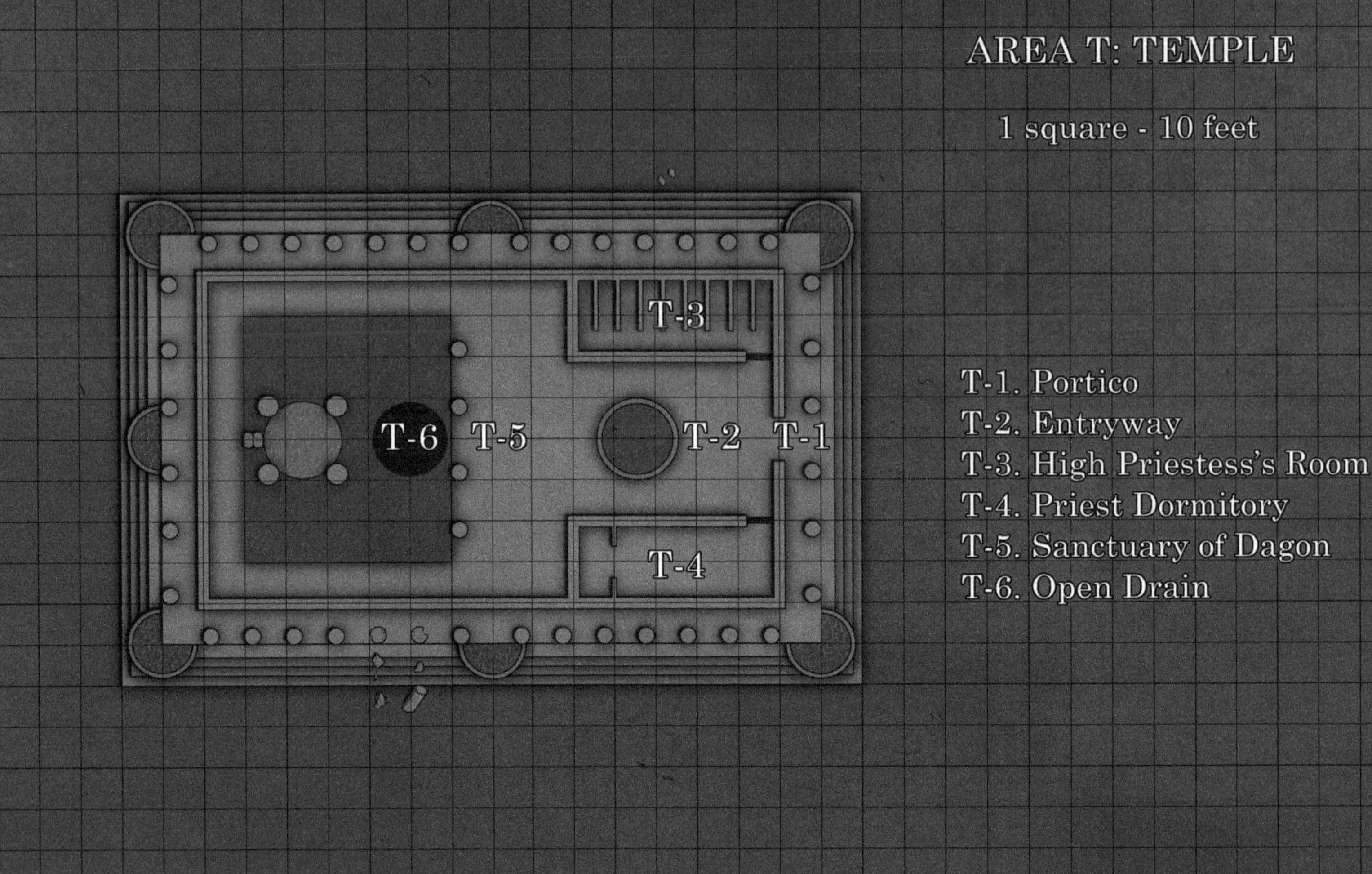

d20	Banes and Boons
1	*Curse*: –6 penalty to random ability*
2	*Destruction*: DC 16 Charisma saving throw or die and rise as a bodak**
3	Random energy vulnerability: cold/fire/acid/force/electricity
4	DC 20 Constitution saving throw or age d10 + 10 years
5	DC 16 Wisdom saving throw or be polymorphed into a giant leech**
6	*Reincarnation*: random race
7	Transformed into a water elemental for 24 hours*
8	Race changes to skum**
9	Random ability score decreases by –1
10	Amorphous form (see **Area R-3. Shrine of Insanity**)
11	Ability score increases by +1 (choose one)
12	Saving throw +1 (choose one)
13	Gain darkvision 60 ft, or increase existing darkvision by 30 ft
14	Add one feat of player's choice that character is eligible for
15	*Reincarnation*: (choose race)
16	Gain proficiency in player's choice of one skill
17	Gain expertise in player's choice of one skill character is proficient in
18	Gain (1d4 + 1)*1000 experience
19+	User's choice (from above options)

* *Greater restoration* to remedy
** See **Appendix A**

T-4. PRIEST DORMITORY

> Messy cots hide behind plain, dirty curtains that divide the space into nine semi-private apartments.

Air-breathing priestly minions of the temple bunk here. Of the eight current **priests**, four are in this room. Four more are in **Area T-5**. These devotees of Dagon are drawn from local island populations, though you could include a half-sea elf or other humanoid race as best fits your game setting. If the priests detect intruders, they suit up for combat and defend the temple.

> These pale, clammy humans bear wicked-looking tridents and bear grim expressions. Their hair is long and unkempt, and their dirty wetsuits are made of studded leather.

If the priests are attacked here, they call out for the guards in the sanctuary. If they hear combat outside this room, they come out to support their comrades.

T-5. Sanctuary of Dagon

A terrible idol of Dagon dominates the tall dais in the center of this magnificent chamber. The figure resembles a writhing mass of barbed, suckered tentacles cloaking a winding, eel-like body. Its head is that of a deep-sea fish with a baleful intelligence. Its toothy maw grins evilly. The ceiling soars to dark mosaics above. Tall support columns resemble bound stalks of seaweed rising from beds of coral. The sanctuary is covered in once beautiful bas-reliefs, but recent additions distort the images. Heads and limbs of figures have been reworked to resemble primordial sea creatures from some nightmarish Abyssal realm. A dark pool of water is before the idol. Four everburning flames in tall decorative braziers light the areas.

The great idol is trapped (see below). The ceiling rises 40 feet above the floor. A **skum guard captain** named Doolkah, 4 **skum** temple guards (with AC 21 from shields, see below), and a **sahuagin priestess** (with *boots of levitation* and a *wand of paralysis*) named Shacilla ring the idol (see **Appendix A** for all three). The skum practice their worship music in the southwest corner of the room on drums, horns, and insanely constructed flutes. The instruments function in air and water environments and are worth 2,000 gp.

The idol is trapped. The trap can be detected with a successful DC 19 Intelligence (Arcana) check. Any living being who touches the idol awakens the Spirit of Dagon, which responds as a *phantasmal killer* spell. The creature must succeed on a DC 17 Wisdom saving throw or become frightened for one minute. A frightened creature takes 33 (6d10) psychic damage at the beginning of each its turns and can attempt a DC 17 Wisdom saving throw at the end of each of its turns to end the frightened condition. The huge Dagonic statue animates like the demon lord himself and attacks! If a *consecrate* spell is cast beforehand, the *phantasmal killer* is negated. Read the following on a fail:

The gargantuan idol animates and reaches out for you, its many unblinking red eyes glaring and tentacles waving. Its maw is full of rows of long fangs, each dripping with slime, as it lunges out to devour you!

Each scowling fish man wears a bronze helmet green with age. They pass a hand over odd-looking, tube-like devices at their hips that are attached by a line to a round metal shield of yellow metal. A magnetic whine begins, and each shield thrums with energy as the warriors draw deadly-looking tridents and take up practiced defensive stances.

The guards carry large round shields made of a special golden metal called orichalcum. Used by the ancients to channel their primordial magical energies, when attached to a special battery these orichalcum shields can raise their defensive capabilities and grant a +3 bonus. The batteries have limited charges. The ones used here have three charges remaining; each charge activates the bonus for one minute. These same batteries can be used to power the wicked machine in **Area T-3**.

All creatures in this room fight bravely. If the temple looks as if it's under serious threat, Underpriestess Shacilla dives into the pool to alert the high priestess.

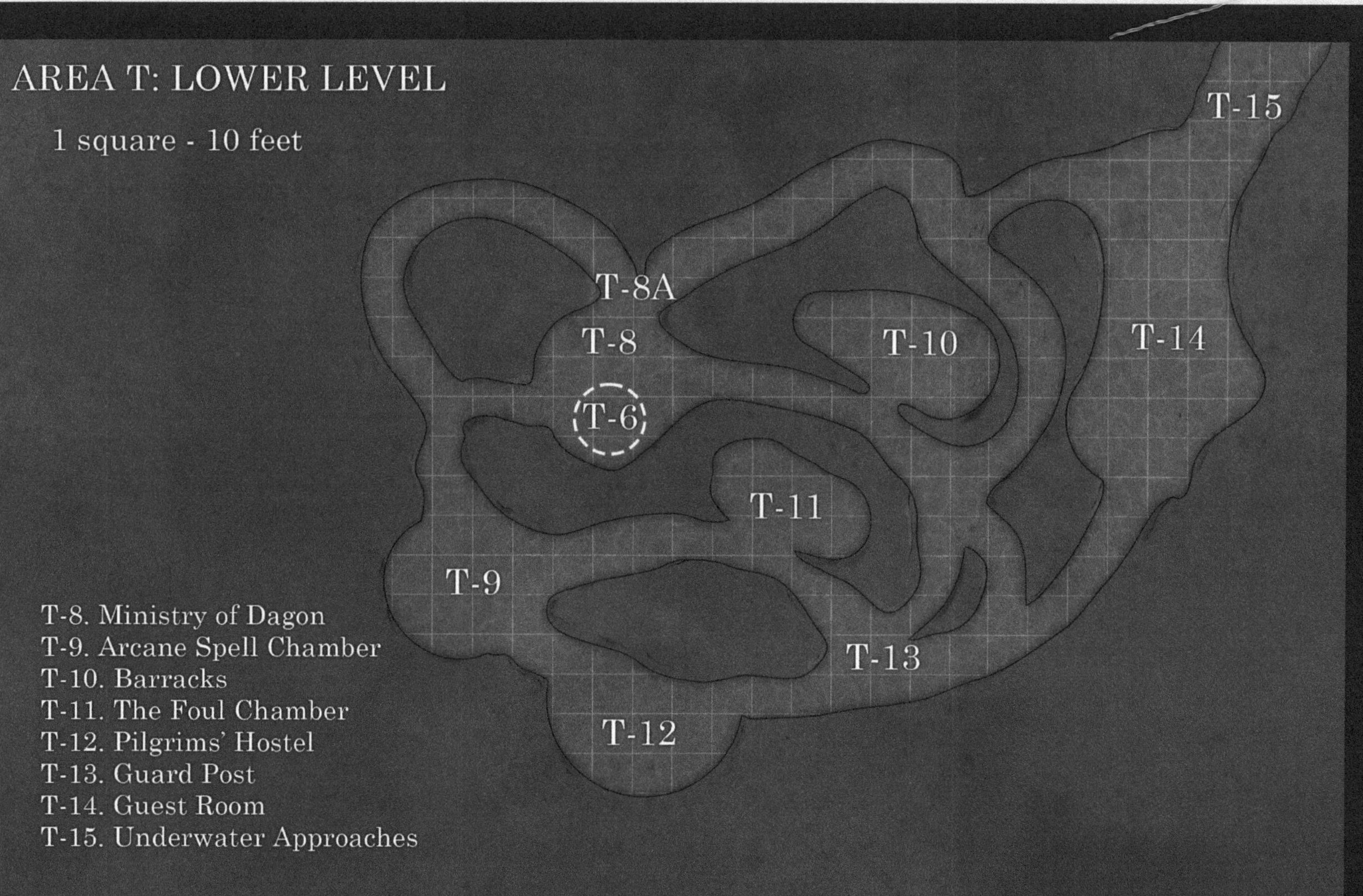

T-6. Vertical Descent Passage

The tube descends 60 feet and opens into the ceiling of the ministry of Dagon (**Area T-8**). About halfway down, a side passage leads to the oratorium (**Area T-7**). Guarding the passage to the oratorium are 2 **chuuls** that attack strangers who enter the vertical passage. They can be spotted with a successful DC 16 Wisdom (Perception) check. The runes carved on the walls are slightly nauseating, but otherwise harmless.

T-7. Oratorium

This encounter can be quite dangerous for an unprepared mid-level party, so carefully monitor their readiness and drop hints if necessary.

Lycinia (See **Appendix A**), the temple's high priestess, spends much of her time in this room scheming and giving speeches to temple attendants (4 **ghouls** with Swim speed 30 feet). Carvings of ancient runes are on the walls of the tubular entryway. They are litanies on the glory of Dagon but are not dangerous. However, a *glyph of warding* is at the threshold of the oratorium. Any non-evil creature who crosses the threshold is affected by *dispel magic*. Make a spell check at +8 to determine what spells and magical effects are affected.

Lycinia is a fanatic and fights to the death.

T-8. Ministry of Dagon

This area includes the intersection at the bottom of the vertical shaft and the tubular passage to the northwest. Dozing here are 2 aquatic **trolls** (add Swim speed 40 feet and the ability to breathe underwater). Ever hungry, they attack any intruders when roused but they retreat to the barracks (**Area T-10**) or the guard post (**Area T-13**) for help if reduced to fewer than half their hit points. They fear the "ministers" to the northwest and the dragon in the guest room (**Area T-14**) and will not trespass in either of those places.

A pair of alien scholars reside down the horseshoe-shaped tubal passageway to the northwest (**T-8A**), where they ponder the foul glories of Dagon. Abominations of mysterious origin, other temple devotees know them as the "ministers of Dagon" though they refer to themselves as **cnidarians** (see **Appendix A**). They resemble enormous jellyfish with prehensile tentacles and throbbing blue brains deep within their blobby bodies. They appear to communicate with each other through hums and vibrations but with other creatures by marking on basalt tablets with a stylus. Though they have yet to produce much of any practical use, Lycinia places a high value on them. Hence, others in the temple give them a wide berth.

The ministers ignore any noises or disturbances outside their passageway. They are far too absorbed in their studies to care. However, if attacked, they respond with *daze* spells and tentacle attacks. Their daze is a kind of overwhelming telepathic feedback to distract and confuse opponents, blasting them with words and information. If attacked from one direction, one of them swims around to the other side and attacks the party from behind.

Seven hand-sized idols of ancient gods expertly carved from coral and worth 50 gp each are on shelf-like niches in the tubular passage. Two of them contain magic liquids: a *potion of barnacleskin* (see **Appendix B**) and a *potion of fins to feet* (see **Appendix B**).

Despite its appearance, the writing on the walls (mostly in Aboleth) is not magical. The glowing letters are achieved using rare undersea pigments. Several rubbings can be obtained from the writing. It takes time (10 minutes per section) but 10 sections can be copied for a trade value of 1,000 gp each.

T-9. Arcane Spell Chamber

This room constitutes a massive arcane spellbook. Druid and clerical spells are also inscribed. Though written in an ancient script, each spell can be accurately interpreted with a successful DC 15 Intelligence (Arcana or Religion) check. If the glyphs are touched, a **trilobite swarm** is summoned (see **Appendix A**). The trapped nature of the glyphs can be noted with a successful DC 16 Intelligence (Investigation) check.

A secret door in the floor can be found with a successful DC 17 Wisdom (Perception) check and opened with a successful DC 20 Intelligence (Investigation) check or Dexterity check with thieves' tools. Beneath is a 30-foot-wide spherical room warded to prevent its single occupant from leaving. This encounter is optional because it is extremely dangerous for a mid-level party. Include it only if you determine it is a fair challenge for the characters.

The Foul Chamber

The high priestess keeps G'zhool, a **hezrou demon**, inside this 30-foot-wide chamber. Summoned for some nefarious future plan, his reeking body is too unpleasant for most of the water-breathing denizens of the temple to endure for long. Thus, he is kept imprisoned in this room. Bored with his detention, the demon happily attacks any intruder foolish enough

to open the door, although he prefers to wait until they enter before attacking. Remember that this room is like a spherical fishbowl entered from above; those who can't swim may sink to the bottom, possibly putting themselves out of melee range. The demon's nausea effect still affects those combatants who use the water for breathing. However, he can't teleport out or summon another demon because of the chamber's wards. He thus fights until he sees an opportunity to charge out of the room. If brought to 0 hit points, he bursts into oily, black slime, leaving only his necklace behind. The room is unremarkable except for the smell. G'zhool wears a surprisingly beautiful gold medallion crafted into a likeness of Dagon (2,000 gp). It hangs around his neck on a chain of thick silver links (1,000 gp).

T-10. Skum Barracks

The room is the bunk space for 6 **skum** temple guards (see **Appendix A**). They switch off with the guards in the main sanctuary (**Area T-1**) or at the guard posts in the lower levels (**Areas T-13** and **T-15**). Those found here are likely sleeping. Each has weapons and armor bound in a nearby net.

T-11. Litharium

To unlock the door, the pieces must be realigned to form the rough image of an aboleth. The opening mechanism requires a successful DC 23 Dexterity check with thieves' tools to decipher. A successful DC 18 Intelligence (Investigation) check gives advantage to the Dexterity check. If unlocked, the stone door rolls to the side and allows entrance. Any failure sets off a trap. The trap can be noted with a successful DC 20 Intelligence (Investigation) check and can only be disarmed by successfully opening the door. If the trap is triggered, jets of freezing water shoot out from the frame of the doorway. Each creature within the chamber must make a DC 16 Dexterity saving throw. A creature that fails takes 10 (3d6) cold damage and is restrained by the ice. A creature that succeeds takes half this damage and is not restrained. A restrained creature can attempt a DC 18 Strength (Athletics) check at the end of each of its turns to escape. If they don't succeed before, the ice releases them after 10 minutes. The water in the chamber is difficult terrain for 20 minutes after the trap is triggered due to the icy sludge, and a creature in the area must make a DC 14 Constitution saving throw each minute or suffer 3 (1d6) cold damage. The trap takes one hour to reset.

The ancients stored their *ioun stones* here. The drawers contain 52 aged stones that are all dull gray. The five stones orbiting the sphere are *sustenance*, *protection*, *strength*, and two dull grays. They can be captured without resistance from the sphere.

Crossbows, bolt cases, tridents, spears, and weapon belts hang from hooks on the walls. Large sewn seaweed duffels used like sleeping bags are lined up at the back of the room.

Camped out in this room are **8 sahuagin** and **2 hunter sharks**. They are waiting to attend the next weekly sacrificial ceremony. They brought a box of treasure and two sea elf captives as offerings to Dagon. The leader also carries a *pearl of the sirens* (see **Appendix B**). A "beastmaster" sahuagin leads his sharks around to the rear of an invading force to attack from behind — alerting temple guards as he finds them. The box is unlocked and contains a variety of valuables from sunken ships (cups, plates, rings, etc.) worth 1,000 gp. Any treasure not part of the ancient site is fair salvage for the party and does not need to be turned in. However, it is still accepted for credit if desired at the same rate.

T-13. Guard Post

The tube-like passage widens and flattens at an intersection. Sections of the wall contain half-completed carvings depicting grotesque sea creatures menacing hapless human swimmers.

Keeping watch at this point are **3 skum** temple guards (see **Appendix A**). One of the guards uses an octopus shield (see **Appendix B**). If they notice a dangerous group of intruders, they retreat to alert the guards in the skum barracks (**Area T-10**) or the high priestess in the oratorium (**Area T-7**).

T-14. Guest Room

Graffiti covers the walls of this enormous cavern where visitors for more than 3,000 years have left testaments of their passing. Recent additions include bizarre antediluvian sea creatures and unidentified humanoid sea inhabitants. A very large black monster is curled up in a meditative pose in the eastern corner of the room.

An **adult black dragon** named Distrattadora recently arrived to pay tribute to Dagon and join the gathering forces for plunder. She is patiently awaiting her audience with the high priestess. If she detects intruders, she is annoyed at the disturbance and the lack of proper security. She breaks her pose and cheerfully blasts the intruders with her breath weapon before entering melee. Remember, a black dragon can breathe underwater indefinitely and can freely use its breath weapon, spells, and other abilities while submerged.

Distrattadora does not believe any intruders could possibly threaten her life, but if she is reduced to 50 or fewer hit points, she roars angrily in hopes of summoning help from the guards at the guard post (**Area T-13**), who arrive in one round. If they see it's hopeless, they retreat to the ministry of Dagon (**Area T-8**) to alert the aquatic trolls and also send one of their number to warn the high priestess (**Area T-7**). See the **Temple Tactics** sidebar for more information.

Distrattadora carries treasure with her in belt bags (7,000 gp in coin, gold jewelry, and pearls). If the ceiling is searched with a successful DC 20 Wisdom (Perception) check, a hovering belt buckle can be found. It is made of orichalcum and functions as an *immovable rod*. Long ago, sculptors used it as a brace for underwater carving. If the belts are reconstructed and the activation words discovered, it functions as a belt that suspends the wearer in any environment.

T-15. Underwater Approach

Colossal megaliths from an enormous, pillared promenade leading up to the temple mount are splayed like fallen timbers from a massive earthquake that sank the ancient city. Sea plants and coral grow like weeds among the wreckage.

Ranging near the underwater entrance are **4 devilfish** (see **Appendix A**) that remain concealed behind a grove of seaweed at the base of the temple mount. They are aggressive and attack suspicious characters. Standing guard just inside the opening are **2 skum** temple guards (see **Appendix**). If faced with a well-armed force, they retreat inside to warn the high priestess. See the **Temple Tactics** sidebar below for more.

Temple Tactics

If the sunken ruins are cleared of monsters before an assault on the temple, then the temple inhabitants are more on their guard. Murder and mayhem is commonplace among the motley assemblage of creatures in the ruins, so minor disturbances go unheeded. As well, defeated denizens of the ruins are also unlikely to report their losses to the high priestess. Chaotic and evil Dagonians are not known for their support and compassion.

The inhabitants of the temple don't just sit around once they become aware that the complex is under attack. If adventurers are noticed entering from the underwater approach passage (**Area T-15**), guards in **Areas T-11** and **T-13** are alerted and one of their number swims off to alert the high priestess (**Area T-7**). She takes her lacedon bodyguards to the bottom of the vertical passage (**Area T-6**), casts her buff spells, and moves to assail the intruders. If hard pressed, Lycinia summons aid from the aquatic trolls and "ministers" in **Area T-8** and directs them to circle around from a new direction to surround the invaders. If possible, she attempts to capture prisoners to interrogate. If alerted that the temple sanctuary (**Areas T-2 through T-5**) is under attack, she casts her buff spells in **Area T-7** and prepares her defenses there. She sends one lacedon to summon the aquatic trolls in **Area T-8** to take a defensive position in the entry hall to the oratorium (**Area T-7**).

TEMPLE OF DAGON

If at any point High Priestess Lycinia is slain, word spreads quickly and her minions in the dungeon or sunken ruins quickly leave the area to seek their fortunes elsewhere. Without a charismatic spiritual leader at the center of the community, the remaining skum and sahuagin break ranks. Human cultists flee in terror, taking anything of value that they can carry. The remaining monsters, including the hag coven and Distrattadora the black dragon, lurk around the complex and can still be encountered.

APPENDIX A: NEW MONSTERS

Allip

Medium undead, chaotic evil

Armor Class 11
Hit Points 33 (6d8 + 6)
Speed fly 30 ft.

STR	DEX	CON	INT	WIS	CHA
6 (−2)	13 (+1)	13 (+1)	11 (+0)	11 (+0)	16 (+3)

Skills Perception +2, Stealth +3
Senses darkvision 60 ft., passive Perception 12
Languages Common, Deep Speech
Challenge 2 (450 XP)

Babble. The allip incoherently mutters to itself, creating a hypnotic effect. All creatures within 30 feet that aren't incapacitated must succeed on a DC 11 Wisdom saving throw. On a failed save, the creature becomes charmed for the duration. While charmed by this spell, the creature is incapacitated and has a speed of 0. The effect ends for an affected creature if it takes any damage or if someone else uses an action to shake the creature out of its stupor.

Incorporeal Movement. The allip can move through other creatures and objects as if they were difficult terrain. It takes 5 (1d10) force damage if it ends its turn inside an object.

Madness. Anyone targeting an allip with a spell or effect that would make direct contact with its tortured mind must succeed on a DC 11 Wisdom saving throw or take 7 (2d6) psychic damage.

ACTIONS

Touch of Insanity. *Melee Weapon Attack:* +3 to hit, reach 5 ft., one target. *Hit:* 8 (2d6 + 1) psychic damage.

Assassin Vine

Large plant, unaligned

Armor Class 13 (natural armor)
Hit Points 85 (10d10 + 30)
Speed 5 ft.

STR	DEX	CON	INT	WIS	CHA
20 (+5)	10 (+0)	16 (+3)	2 (−4)	13 (+1)	9 (−1)

Damage Resistances cold, fire
Damage Immunities lightning
Senses blindsight 30 ft., passive Perception 11
Languages —
Challenge 4 (1,100 XP)

ACTIONS

Multiattack. The assassin vine can make two melee attacks: two slams or one slam and one constrict.

Slam. *Melee Weapon Attack:* +7 to hit, reach 10 ft., one target. *Hit:* 14 (2d8 + 5) bludgeoning damage. The target is grappled (escape DC 15) if the assassin vine isn't already grappling a creature. The grappled target is restrained until the grapple ends.

Constrict. *Melee Weapon Attack:* +7 to hit, reach 5 ft., one creature grappled by the assassin vine. *Hit:* 18 (3d8 + 5) bludgeoning damage.

Bodak

Medium undead, chaotic evil

Armor Class 16 (natural armor)
Hit Points 120 (16d8 + 48)
Speed 30 ft.

STR	DEX	CON	INT	WIS	CHA
18 (+4)	18 (+4)	16 (+3)	6 (−2)	14 (+2)	10 (+0)

Saving Throws Con +7, Wis +6
Skills Perception +6, Stealth +8
Damage Resistances acid, fire, necrotic; bludgeoning, piercing, and slashing from nonmagical attacks
Damage Immunities lightning, poison
Condition Immunities charmed, frightened, poisoned
Senses darkvision 120 ft., passive Perception 16
Languages Abyssal, Common.
Challenge 9 (5,000 XP)

Aura of Obliteration. The bodak is surrounded by an annihilating aura of obliteration. All creatures other than undead and fiends that start their turn within 30 feet of the bodak take 9 (2d8) necrotic damage. The bodak can emit or suppress this aura using a bonus action.

Gaze of Orcus. If a creature starts its turn within 30 ft. of the bodak and the two of them can see each other, the bodak can force the creature to make a DC 12 Constitution saving throw if the bodak isn't incapacitated. On a failed save, the creature drops to 0 hit points, unless it is immune to the frightened condition. On a success, the creature takes 22 (4d10) psychic damage. A creature that is slain by the bodak's Gaze rises as a bodak 24 hours later unless restored to life by magical means.

A creature that isn't surprised can avert its eyes to avoid the saving throw at the start of its turn. If it does so, it can't see the bodak until the start of its next turn, when it can avert its eyes again. If it looks at the bodak in the meantime, it must immediately make the save.

Sunlight Antipathy. The bodak takes 5 radiant damage when it starts its turn in sunlight. While in sunlight, it has disadvantage on attack rolls and ability checks.

ACTIONS

Multiattack. The bodak uses its Scornful Glare and makes two Slam attacks.

Slam. *Melee Weapon Attack:* +8 to hit, reach 5 ft., one creature. *Hit:* 8 (1d8 + 4) bludgeoning damage and 13 (3d8) necrotic damage.

***Scornful Glare* (recharge 4–6)**. The bodak targets one creature it can see within 60 feet of it. If the target can see the bodak, it must attempt a DC 12 Wisdom saving throw. The creature takes 22 (4d10) necrotic damage and is frightened for 1 minute on a failed save. On a successful save, the creature takes half as much damage and is not frightened.

Caryatid Column

Medium construct, unaligned

Armor Class 14 (natural armor)
Hit Points 45 (6d8 + 18)
Speed 20 ft.

STR	DEX	CON	INT	WIS	CHA
16 (+3)	14 (+2)	16 (+3)	2 (−4)	11 (+0)	1 (−5)

Damage Resistances piercing and slashing damage from nonmagical weapons that aren't adamantine
Damage Immunities poison, psychic
Condition Immunities charmed, exhaustion, frightened, paralyzed, petrified, poisoned
Senses darkvision 120 ft., passive Perception 10
Languages understands the languages of its creator but can't speak
Challenge 2 (450 XP)

Immutable Form. The caryatid column is immune to any spell or effect that would alter its form.

Magic Resistance. The caryatid column has advantage on saving throws against spells and other magical effects.

Magic Weapons. The caryatid column's weapon attacks are magical.

Shatter Weapons. Whenever a character with a weapon strikes a caryatid column with a non-adamantine, nonmagical weapon, the character must succeed on a DC 14 Strength saving throw or the weapon shatters into pieces.

Actions

Longsword. *Melee Weapon Attack:* +5 to hit, reach 5 ft., one target. *Hit:* 8 (1d10 + 3) slashing damage.

Dagon High Priestess

Medium monstrosity, chaotic evil

Armor Class 19 (natural armor and +2 shield)
Hit Points 112 (15d8 + 45)
Speed 30 ft., swim 40 ft.

STR	DEX	CON	INT	WIS	CHA
14 (+2)	15 (+2)	16 (+3)	13 (+1)	16 (+3)	15 (+2)

Skills Deception +6, Insight +7, Medicine +7, Perception +7, Persuasion +6, Religion +5, Stealth +6
Damage Resistances bludgeoning, piercing, and slashing from nonmagical attacks
Senses darkvision 60 ft., passive Perception 17
Languages Aquan, Common, Deep Speech, Sahuagin
Challenge 9 (5,000 XP)

All Around Vision. The Dagon high priestess can't be surprised.

Petrifying Gaze. When a creature which can see the Dagon high priestess's eyes starts its turn within 30 feet of the Dagon high priestess, she can force the target to make a DC 15 Constitution saving throw if the Dagon high priestess isn't incapacitated and can see the target. If the saving throw fails by 5 or more the target is instantly petrified. Otherwise on a failed save, the target magically begins to turn to stone and is restrained. It must repeat the saving throw at the end of its next turn. On a success, the effect ends. On a failure, the target is petrified until freed by the *greater restoration* spell or other magic. A target that isn't surprised can avert its eyes to avoid the saving throw at the start of its turn. If it does so, it can't see the Dagon high priestess until the start of its next turn, when it can avert its eyes again. If it looks at the Dagon high priestess in the meantime, it must immediately make the save. If the Dagon high priestess sees herself on a polished surface within 30 feet of her and in an area of bright light the Dagon high priestess is, due to her curse, affected by her own gaze.

Spellcasting. The Dagon high priestess is a 7th-level spellcaster. Her spellcasting ability is Wisdom (spell save DC 15, +7 to hit with spell attacks). The Dagon high priestess has the following spells prepared:
Cantrips (at will): *light, resistance, sacred flame*
1st level (4 slots): *cure wounds, detect magic, guidance, shield of faith*
2nd level (3 slots): *lesser restoration, spiritual weapon* (trident)
3rd level (3 slots): *dispel magic, water walk*
4th level (1 slot): *control water*

Actions

Multiattack. The Dagon high priestess makes one Snake Hair attack and two Trident attacks.

Snake Hair. *Melee Weapon Attack:* +6 to hit, reach 5 ft., one target. *Hit:* 4 (1d4 + 2) piercing damage and 14 (4d6) poison damage.

+1 Trident. *Melee or Ranged Weapon Attack:* +7 to hit, reach 5 ft., or range 20/60 ft., one target. *Hit:* 6 (1d6 + 3) piercing damage or 6 (1d8 +2) if used two-handed to make a melee attack.

Devilfish

Large fiend, unaligned, chaotic evil

Armor Class 17 (natural armor)
Hit Points 42 (5d10 + 15)
Speed 10 ft., swim 40 ft.

STR	DEX	CON	INT	WIS	CHA
17 (+3)	17 (+3)	16 (+3)	3 (-4)	12 (+1)	8 (-1)

Skills Acrobatics +5, Perception +3
Damage Resistances cold
Condition Immunities prone
Senses darkvision 60 ft., passive Perception 13
Languages Abyssal, Aquan, Common
Challenge 3 (700 XP)

Unholy Blood. A devilfish's blood is infused with fiendish magic. Once per day, as a bonus action, a devilfish can emit a night-black cloud of this foul liquid, filling a 20-foot-radius cloud if underwater, or a 20-foot-radius burst on land. In water, the blood provides total concealment for everything but a devilfish (which can see through the blood with ease); on land the slippery blood coats the ground, making the area difficult terrain. The blood persists for 1 minute before fading. Anyone who enters a cloud of the blood in the water or who is within the area of a burst of blood on land must make a DC 16 Constitution saving throw or be poisoned. A creature can repeat the saving throw at the end of each of its turn ending the effect on a success. A creature who succeeds on the saving throw or who has the effect end for it is immune to the effect from the cloud.

Actions

Multiattack. The Devilfish makes three Tentacle attacks.
Savage Bite. *Melee Weapon Attack:* +6 to hit, reach 5 ft., one target. *Hit:* 9 (2d6 + 3) slashing damage and the target must succeed on a DC 16 Constitution saving throw or take an additional 4 (1d8) poisoned damage and be stunned until the start of the devilfish's next turn. If the attack roll was an 18–20, the target takes an additional 7 (2d6) slashing damage.
Tentacle. *Melee Weapon Attack:* +6 to hit, reach 5 ft., one target. *Hit:* 10 (2d6 + 3) slashing damage and the target must succeed on a DC 16 Dexterity saving throw or be grappled. If the devilfish grapples an opponent, it may use its bonus action to attempt to make a Savage Bite on that opponent.

Eye of the Deep

Medium aberration, lawful evil

Armor Class 14 (natural armor)
Hit Points 117 (18d8 + 36)
Speed 5 ft., swim 20 ft.

STR	DEX	CON	INT	WIS	CHA
14 (+2)	10 (+0)	14 (+2)	12 (+1)	13 (+1)	13 (+1)

Skills Perception +4
Senses darkvision 60 ft., passive Perception 14
Languages Aquan, Common, Deep Speech
Challenge 5 (1,800 XP)

Amphibious. The eye of the deep can breathe in both air and water.
Flyby. The eye of the deep doesn't provoke an opportunity attack when it flies out of an enemy's reach.
Hyper-Awareness. An eye of the deep's eye stalks allow it to see in all directions at once. It cannot be surprised.
Stun Cone. An eye of the deep's central eye produces a cone extending straight ahead from its front to a range of 30 feet. At the start of each of its turns, the eye of the deep decides which way the cone faces and whether the cone is active. All creatures in this area must succeed on a DC 15 Constitution saving throw or be stunned for 1 minute. A creature can repeat the saving throw at the end of each of its turns, ending the effect on itself on a success.

Actions

Multiattack. The eye of the deep makes one Bite attack and two with its Pincers.
Bite. *Melee Weapon Attack:* +5 to hit, reach 5 ft., one target. *Hit:* 12 (3d6 + 2) piercing damage.
Pincers. *Melee Weapon Attack:* +5 to hit, reach 5 ft., one target. *Hit:* 15 (3d8 + 2) bludgeoning damage. The target is grappled (escape DC 12) if the eye of the deep isn't already grappling a creature, and the target is restrained until the grapple ends.
Eye Rays. Each of the creature's eyes stalks can produce a magical ray once per round. The creature can aim both of its eye rays in any direction and they have a range of 150 feet.
Paralytic Ray. Using its left eye, the eye of the deep unleashes a powerful paralytic beam. The target must make a DC 15 Wisdom saving throw or be paralyzed for 1 minute. A creature can repeat the saving throw at the end of each of its turns, ending the effect on itself on a success.

Enfeeblement Ray. Using its right eye, the eye of the deep unleashes a powerful ray of enfeeblement. The target must make a DC 15 Wisdom saving throw or deal half damage with all attacks that use Strength for 1 minute. A creature can repeat the saving throw at the end of each of its turns, ending the effect on itself on a success.
Major Image. The eye of the deep concentrates its eye rays together to project a *major image* illusion. The illusion is generated at any point within range and in the eye of the deep's line of sight. Seeing through the illusion requires a successful DC 15 Intelligence (Investigation) check.

Cnidarian

Large aberration, chaotic evil

Armor Class 14 (natural armor)
Hit Points 90 (20d8)
Speed swim 10 ft.

STR	DEX	CON	INT	WIS	CHA
12 (+1)	12 (+1)	10 (+0)	15 (+2)	10 (+0)	2 (–4)

Senses tremorsense 60 ft. (under water only), passive Perception 10
Challenge 2 (450 XP)
Poison. Any living target damaged by the cnidarian's tentacle attack must make a DC 12 Constitution saving throw or be poisoned for 1d4 hours.
Reactive Tentacles. If a creature moves within 15 feet of a cnidarian, the cnidarian can use its reaction to make a Daze attack.

Actions

Daze. *Melee Weapon Attack:* +3 to hit, reach 15 ft., one target. *Hit:* target is stunned until the beginning of the target's next turn.
Jet. The cnidarian moves directly backward at a speed equal to four times its swim speed. It must move in a straight line and this action does not provoke attacks of opportunity.
Tentacles. *Melee Weapon Attack:* +3 to hit, reach 10 ft., one target. *Hit:* 13 (3d8) poison damage plus poison.

Giant Blowfish

Large beast, unaligned

Armor Class 16 (natural armor)
Hit Points 59 (7d10 + 21)
Speed Swim 30 ft.

STR	DEX	CON	INT	WIS	CHA
17 (+3)	13 (+1)	17 (+3)	1 (-5)	14 (+2)	12 (+1)

Skills Perception +4
Senses darkvision 30 ft., passive Perception 14
Languages —
Challenge 1 (200 XP)

Quills. Any creature attacking a giant blowfish from within 5 feet takes 4 (1d8) piercing damage. A creature that grapples a giant blowfish takes 7 (2d6) piercing damage each round it does so. Creatures damaged by a giant blowfish's quills must succeed on a DC 14 Constitution saving throw or be paralyzed until the start of their next turn.

Actions

Slam. *Melee Weapon Attack:* +5 to hit, reach 5 ft., one target. *Hit:* 10 (2d6 + 3) piercing damage and the target must make a DC 14 Constitution saving throw. A target that fails is poisoned for one minute. While it is poisoned, it is paralyzed and if it is holding its breath, must succeed on an additional DC 14 Constitution saving throw or release its breath. A poisoned creature may attempt another saving throw at the end of each of its turns, ending the effects on a successful save.

Giant Leech

Medium beast (aquatic), unaligned

Armor Class 11
Hit Points 26 (4d8 + 8)
Speed 5 ft., swim 20 ft.

STR	DEX	CON	INT	WIS	CHA
11 (+0)	12 (+1)	14 (+2)	2 (–4)	10 (+0)	1 (–5)

Senses blindsight 30 ft., passive Perception 10
Languages —
Challenge 1 (200 XP)

Amphibious. The giant leech can breathe on both air and water.
Vulnerability to Salt. A handful of salt burns a giant leech as if it were a flask of acid, causing 1d6 acid damage per use.

Actions

Blood Drain. *Melee Weapon Attack:* +3 to hit, reach 5 ft. one creature. Hit: 4 (1d6 + 1) piercing damage, and the leech attaches to the target. While attached, the leech doesn't attack. Instead, at the start of the leech's turns, the target loses 5 (1d8 + 1) hit points due to blood loss.
The leech can detach itself by spending 5 feet of its movement. It does so after it drains 25 hit points of blood from the target or the target dies. A creature, including the target, can use its action to make a DC 10 Strength check to rip the leech off and make it detach.

Giant Moray Eel

Large beast, unaligned

Armor Class 17 (natural armor)
Hit Points 68 (8d10 + 24)
Speed swim 30 ft.

STR	DEX	CON	INT	WIS	CHA
20 (+5)	14 (+2)	16 (+3)	1 (-5)	12 (+1)	8 (-1)

Skills Athletics +8, Perception +7, Stealth +5
Condition Immunities frightened, prone
Senses tremorsense 30 ft., passive Perception 17
Languages —
Challenge 3 (700 XP)

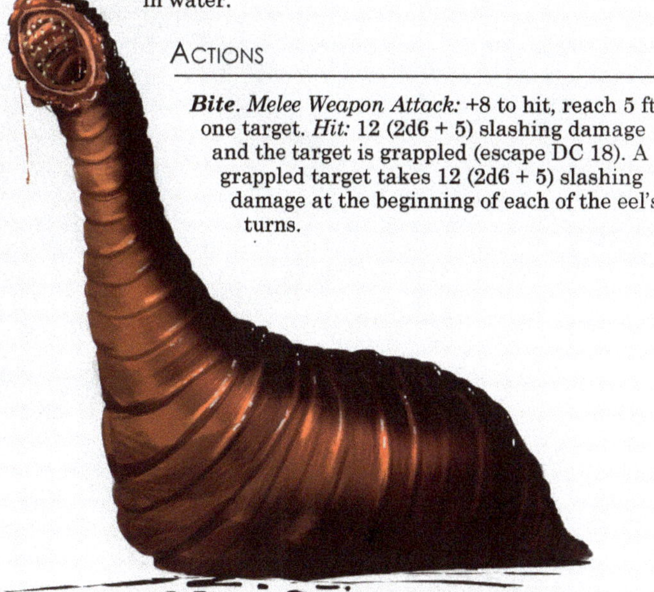

Water Breathing. The giant moral eel can only breathe in water.

Actions

Bite. *Melee Weapon Attack:* +8 to hit, reach 5 ft., one target. *Hit:* 12 (2d6 + 5) slashing damage and the target is grappled (escape DC 18). A grappled target takes 12 (2d6 + 5) slashing damage at the beginning of each of the eel's turns.

Giant Sea Anemone

Large beast, unaligned

Armor Class 14 (natural armor)
Hit Points 38 (4d10 + 16)
Speed swim 5 ft.

STR	DEX	CON	INT	WIS	CHA
12 (+1)	15 (+2)	18 (+4)	1 (-5)	10 (+0)	2 (-4)

Damage Immunities poison
Condition Immunities blinded, charmed, frightened, prone
Senses tremorsense 30 ft., passive Perception 10
Languages —
Challenge 2 (450 XP)

Amorphous. The giant sea anemone can move through a space as narrow as 1 foot wide without squeezing.

Water Breathing. The giant sea anemone can only live underwater.

Sightless. The giant sea anemone does not see and is immune to attacks that depend upon being seen.

Actions

Multiattack. The giant sea anemone makes two tentacle attacks.

Swallow. If the giant sea anemone starts its turn with a Medium or smaller creature grappled in one of its tentacles, it may attempt to swallow the creature. The target must succeed on a DC 14 Dexterity saving throw or be swallowed. A swallowed creature is grappled and restrained and takes 4 (1d6 + 1) bludgeoning damage at the start of each of the anemone's turns. If the anemone is brought to 0 hit points, a swallowed creature may use its movement to escape, ending in an unoccupied square adjacent to the anemone.

Tentacle. *Melee Weapon Attack:* +4 to hit, reach 15 ft., one target. *Hit:* 9 (2d6 + 2) piercing damage and the target is grappled (escape DC 14) and must succeed on a DC 14 Constitution saving throw or take an additional 4 (1d8) poison damage and be poisoned. A poisoned creature can repeat the saving throw at the end of each of its turns, ending the condition on a success.

Anchor. The giant sea anemone anchors itself to a solid surface. While anchored, it has a movement of zero and it has advantage on any saving throw or ability check to avoid being moved.

Lacedon

Medium undead, chaotic evil

Armor Class 11
Hit Points 27 (6d8)
Speed 30 ft., swim 30 ft.

STR	DEX	CON	INT	WIS	CHA
15 (+2)	12 (+1)	10 (+0)	7 (–2)	10 (+0)	6 (–2)

Damage Immunities poison
Condition Immunities charmed, exhaustion, poisoned
Senses darkvision 60 ft., passive Perception 10
Languages Common
Challenge 1 (200 XP)

Amphibious. The lacedon can breathe air and water.

Actions

Claws. *Melee Weapon Attack:* +3 to hit, reach 5 ft., one target. *Hit:* 7 (2d4 + 2) slashing damage. If the target is a creature other than an elf or undead, it must succeed on a DC 10 Constitution saving throw or be paralyzed for 1 minute. The target can repeat the saving throw at the end of each of its turns, ending the effect on itself on a success.

Spined Fins (recharge 6). The lacedon flexes the spined fins on its arms and swings its arms outward. Up to three creatures within 10 feet of the lacedon must make a DC 12 Dexterity saving throw, taking 7 (2d6) piercing damage on a failed save, or half as much damage on a successful one. If a creature is paralyzed because of the lacedon's claws, the creature must succeed on a DC 10 Constitution saving throw or also take 4 (1d8) poison damage.

Sahuagin Priestess

Medium humanoid (sahuagin), lawful evil

Armor Class 12 (natural armor)
Hit Points 33 (6d8 + 6)
Speed 30 ft., swim 40 ft.

STR	DEX	CON	INT	WIS	CHA
13 (+1)	11 (+0)	12 (+1)	12 (+1)	14 (+2)	13 (+1)

Skills Perception +6, Religion +3
Senses darkvision 120 ft., passive Perception 16
Languages Sahuagin, Aquan
Challenge 2 (450 XP)

Blood Frenzy. The sahuagin priestess has advantage on melee attack rolls against any creature that doesn't have all its hit points.

Limited Amphibiousness. The sahuagin priestess can breathe air and water but begins to suffocate if not submerged at least once every 4 hours.

Saltwater Sensitivity. While completely submerged in saltwater, the sahuagin priestess has advantage on Wisdom (Perception) checks that rely on hearing.

Shark Telepathy. The sahuagin priestess can magically command any shark within 120 feet of her, using a limited telepathy.

Spellcasting. The sahuagin priestess is a 6th-level spellcaster. Her spellcasting ability is Wisdom (spell save DC 12, +4 to hit with spell attacks). She has the following cleric spells prepared:

Cantrips (at will): *guidance, thaumaturgy*
1st level (4 slots): *bless, detect magic, guiding* bolt
2nd level (3 slots): *hold person, spiritual weapon* (trident)
3rd level (3 slots): *mass healing word, tongues*

Actions

Multiattack. The sahuagin makes one Bite attack and one with her Claws.

Bite. *Melee Weapon Attack:* +3 to hit, reach 5 ft., one target. *Hit:* 3 (1d4 + 1) piercing damage.

Claws. *Melee Weapon Attack:* +3 to hit, reach 5 ft., one target. *Hit:* 3 (1d4 + 1) slashing damage.

Skum

Medium monstrosity, lawful evil

Armor Class 16 (natural armor)
Hit Points 27 (5d8 + 5)
Speed 30 ft., swim 40 ft.

STR	DEX	CON	INT	WIS	CHA
15 (+2)	14 (+2)	13 (+1)	8 (–1)	11 (+0)	9 (–1)

Skills Perception +2, Stealth +6
Senses darkvision 60 ft., passive Perception 12
Languages Undercommon, Aboleth
Challenge 1 (200 XP)

Limited Amphibiousness. The skum can breathe air and water but begins to suffocate if not submerged at least once every 4 hours.

Actions

Multiattack. The skum makes one Trident attack, one Bite attack, and one Claws attack.

Trident. *Melee or Ranged Weapon Attack:* +4 to hit, reach 5 ft. or range 20/60/ft., one creature. *Hit:* 6 (1d8 + 2) piercing damage.

Bite. *Melee Weapon Attack:* +4 to hit, reach 5 ft., one creature. *Hit:* 5 (1d6 + 2) piercing damage.

Claws. *Melee Weapon Attack:* +4 to hit, reach 5 ft., one creature. *Hit:* 6 (1d8 + 2) slashing damage.

Skum Guard Captain

Medium monstrosity, lawful evil

Armor Class 22 (plate armor and +2 shield)
Hit Points 75 (10d8 + 30)
Speed 15 ft., swim 40 ft.

STR	DEX	CON	INT	WIS	CHA
16 (+3)	13 (+1)	17 (+3)	10 (+0)	10 (+0)	6 (–2)

Skills Perception +3, Stealth +4
Damage Resistances cold
Senses darkvision 60 ft., passive Perception 13
Languages Aquan, Deep Speech
Challenge 5 (1,800 XP)

Brave. The skum guard captain has advantage on saving throws against being frightened.

Limited Amphibiousness. The skum guard captain can breathe air and water but begins to suffocate if not submerged at least once every 4 hours.

Magic Weapons. The skum guard captain's weapon attacks are magical.

Phalanx Formation. The skum guard captain has advantage on attack rolls and Dexterity saving throws while standing within 5 feet of an ally wielding a shield. In addition, while wielding a shield, the skum guard captain can use a two-handed polearm.

Special Equipment. The skum guard captain is equipped with a *potion of greater healing*, a *+2 shield*, and *mariner's armor* (plate).

Actions

Multiattack. The skum guard captain makes three pike attacks.

Pike. *Melee Weapon Attack:* +6 to hit, reach 5 ft., one target. *Hit:* 10 (2d6 + 3) slashing damage.

Reactions

Saving Shield. When a creature the skum guard captain can see attacks a target within 5 feet of the captain, the captain can use its reaction to impose disadvantage on the roll.

Swarm Of Trilobites

Small swarm of tiny beasts, unaligned

Armor Class 17 (natural armor)
Hit Points 22 (5d6 + 5)
Speed 30 ft., swim 50 ft.

STR	DEX	CON	INT	WIS	CHA
3 (–4)	14 (+2)	13 (+1)	1 (–5)	10 (+0)	2 (–4)

Condition Immunities charmed, exhaustion, frightened, prone
Senses darkvision 60 ft.
Languages —
Challenge 1/4 (50 XP)

Swarm. The swarm of trilobites can occupy another creature's space and vice versa, and the swarm of trilobites can move through any opening large enough for a trilobite. The swarm of trilobites can't regain hit points or gain temporary hit points.

Water Breathing. The swarm of trilobites can breathe only underwater.

Actions

Bite. *Melee Weapon Attack:* +4 to hit, reach 5 ft., one target. *Hit:* 9 (2d6 + 2) piercing damage.

APPENDIX B: EQUIPMENT & MAGIC ITEMS

Listed below are new mundane and magical items found in this adventure:

CARPET OF HOLDING

Wondrous item, rare

A carpet of holding appears to be a five-foot-by-10-foot area rug with ornate designs. If an item is placed on the carpet and the carpet is then folded or rolled up, the item shifts into a nondimensional space capable of holding up to 1,000 pounds and 150 cubic feet. When the command word is spoken and the carpet unfolded, the contents appear again just as they were before. If the carpet is merely unfolded without speaking the command word, it appears and functions as an ordinary carpet, at which point new objects up to the maximum weight may be added as desired.

A living creature placed within the closed carpet can survive for up to 10 minutes, after which time they suffocate. If a *carpet of holding* is placed within a *portable hole*, a rift to the Astral Plane is torn asunder in the space. The carpet and the *portable hole* are sucked into the void and lost forever. Attempting to place a *portable hole* or a *bag of holding* in a folded *carpet of holding* repels the magic items away from the carpet with magnetic force and prevents the carpet from closing.

DECANTER OF ENDLESS AIR

Wondrous item, rare

This stoppered flask weighs about 1 pound. You can use an action to remove the stopper and speak one of three command words, where upon a quantity of fresh air comes streaming out. The air stops flowing at the start of your next turn. Choose from the following options:
- "Breath" produces enough air for you to breathe deeply, filling your lungs.
- "Gust" produces a 10-foot stream of air that is strong enough to extinguish small flames, fan large flames, and move light objects.
- "Tempest" produces a powerful wind that is 30 feet long and one foot wide. As a bonus action while holding the decanter, you can aim the wind at a creature you can see within 30 feet of you. The target must succeed on a DC 13 Strength saving throw or take 1d4 bludgeoning damage and fall prone. Instead, you can target an object that isn't being worn or carried and that weighs no more than 200 pounds. The object is either knocked over or pushed up to 15 feet away from you.

HELM OF WATER BREATHING

Wondrous item, uncommon

While wearing this helm underwater, you can use an action to speak its command word. When you do, the helm provides you with air to breathe. It continues to provide you with fresh air until you speak the command word again, the helm is removed, or you are no longer underwater.

OCTOPUS SHIELD

Armor (shield), very rare requires attunement)

This round, heavy bronze and steel shield is fashioned to resemble a raging octopus. You gain a +2 bonus to your armor class in addition to the shield's normal bonus. Three times per day you can use a bonus action to command the shield's tentacles to animate in a grapple attempt. The shield makes Strength (Athletics) check with a bonus equal to 4 plus your proficiency modifier.

PEARL OF THE SIRENS

Wondrous item, uncommon

While holding this pearl in your hand, you can breathe underwater, you have a swim speed of 60 feet, and you can cast spells and act underwater without hindrance.

POTION OF BARNACLESKIN

Potion, uncommon

When you use an action to drink this potion, your skin becomes covered in barnacles. If you are not wearing armor, you gain a +2 bonus to your armor class. The potion lasts for one hour.

POTION OF FINS TO FEET

Potion, rare

When you use an action to drink this potion, you gain the ability to breathe air and you can transform your body to have humanoid legs. You gain a walking speed equal to your swim speed. The potion lasts for 4 hours.

APPENDIX C: ACCOUNTING LEDGER

MASTER ADVENTURER:

Item:	Credit	Debit	Balance

BOUNTY

IN GOLD *For The Heads Of*
PIRATES

Attacking Trade Ships

&

Murdering Our People!

Our honorable High Judge

Percutio Opavian

Will issue

Letters of marque

To

Heroic Corsairs

Who take up the sword against our enemies

Present this notice to the Judicial Palace